I0646585

The extraordinary tales of

Queenie Alice Moon

Evil Flying Snakes
Steal Happiness

Jo Brothers
Illustrated by Lovee

The Extraordinary Tales of Queenie Alice Moon - Evil Flying Snakes Steal Hapiness

Second Printing, 2015
Text and Artwork Copyright © 2015 Jo Brothers
ISBN 978-0-9922538-8-2

Published by:
Perpetuity Media
PO Box 4444
Shortland Street
Auckland
New Zealand 1140

www.perpetuitymedia.com

Published in New Zealand

Printed in the United States of America

Everyone has
extraordinary tales to tell.

This book is dedicated to
you.

Queenie Alice Moon together with her parents King Leo and Queen Arabella and her magical guardians, Moonbeam the Unicorn, Yang the Dragon and Pugnatius the Pug were all in the Hall of Magic having a meeting.

The Hall of Magic was a hall that ran throughout the entire Palace and the hall had ears. It had recorded all previous conversations that had been conducted in the hall across all of time.

"We have had a serious breach in security in the west fields of the Palace. Somehow an evil army of flying snakes have broken into our sacred land of Spectrum and have stolen happiness!" announced Leo with a serious look on his face.

Queenie, Moonbeam, Yang and Pugnatius all gasped in horror! Yang the Dragon blew a dragon breath hologram that showed them what had happened and it was not a pretty sight.

Thousands of yellow and black bumble bees, flower fairies and coloured butterflies had lost their happiness. Nature and Mother Earth work in harmony to support the Worlds and Kingdoms we live in, so that we can enjoy our lives.

Now that the bumble bees, flower fairies and butterflies were sad, they were transmitting sad energy and all the Worlds and Kingdoms were sad.

We are all connected.

Queenie said "We must transform this dastardly situation! I know let's sing and dance to generate and restore happiness to show all the people and creatures of Mother Earth some love!"

"What a wonderful idea!" said Pugnatius.

King Leo and Queen Arabella looked at each other and smiled in agreement the way parents do. Moonbeam was so excited that he smiled and a rainbow of magic poured out of his horn.

"Quick, lets get down to the gardens at once!" Queenie said. In such times of urgent action, Queenie was allowed to use her magic abilities.

Queenie closed her eyes and imagined herself, Pugnatius, Moonbeam and Yang being magically transported to the centre of the garden by the water fountain.

They arrived in a flash of magic yellow mist.

Queenie gasped, Pugnatius snorted, Moonbeam was silent and Yang froze in mid air. They could not believe what they saw.

There were butterflies flying slowly, sleepy bumble bees tasting the nectar from sad droopy flowers and the flower fairies were standing on the ground unable to fly.

Bluebelle, one of the flower fairies, looked at Queenie and she sobbed "Please help us Queenie!"

Queenie thought for a moment and her golden Crown of Wisdom shone brightly.

"Let's make some happiness to generate happy energy! Come on everyone, let us sing, dance and smile to let happiness reign!" Queenie said with a happy smile on her face.

Queenie started to dance in circles, laughing with happiness. All at once Yang, Moonbeam and Pugnatius joined in dancing, singing and being happy.

Then something wonderful happened, Pugnatius started to sing and he had a beautiful voice that echoed across the Kingdoms and everyone smiled.

A miracle happened, flowers started to glow brightly, bumble bees started to fly again and humming birds came to dance.

Flowers glowed in beautiful bright colours and butterflies came out of their cocoons. The Palace Gardens were ALIVE with happiness.

What an inspirational moment, to see everyone working together to create such an amazing positive change.

Queenie wanted to make an announcement, so she jumped up on a chocolate rock and said "Remember no one can take something from you that is yours! Happiness is a choice and it cannot be taken from us".

As everyone continued to dance and sing and be happy, an incredible energy of happiness and joy flowed out of the Palace Gardens and into the Worlds and Kingdoms.

The energy of love and happiness flowed out into the Worlds and Kingdoms like a ripple effect to find other people and places in need of love, joy and happiness.

Queenie, Moonbeam, Yang and Pugnatius stayed in the Palace Gardens for hours feeling happy that their sharing and caring actions had helped restore happiness to the Worlds and Kingdoms.

The bumblebees, flower fairies and flowers asked Queenie "What happens to the happiness that was stolen by the evil flying snakes?"

Queenie replied "It is already back with us. Happiness is infinite, we can create as much happiness as we like. The evil flying snakes wanted to make us sad. However, working in unity together, we have created even stronger happiness than before!"

Queenie wants to know "What can you do today to bring happiness to someone?"

About Jo

Jo has a passion for storytelling and writing that started when she was a young girl and continues to this very day. She has a vivid imagination and loves creating new worlds and wonderful characters that burst into life with valour and flamboyance such as Queenie Alice Moon and Nano the Robot.

She equally writes intriguing novelettes with quirky, eccentric characters that are weaved into supernatural themes and in her soon to be released books series, Immortales Excelsus she writes about an ordinary, thoroughly bored teen, Sabra Leon, who discovers she and her family are not so ordinary and that their history has more than a few secrets that date back to the dawn of time.

"Thanks for visiting, happy imagining! "

Please keep in touch with me at www.jobrothers.com

Jo lives in Auckland, New Zealand with her husband Sean, in a home filled with books and imagination.